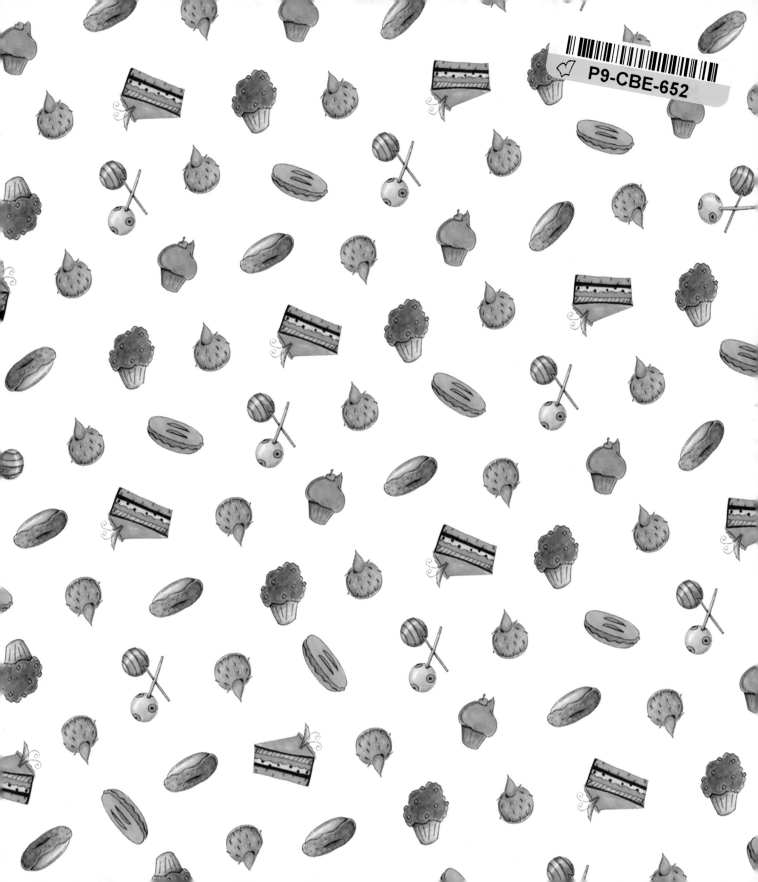

The Good Dog

and the Bad Cat

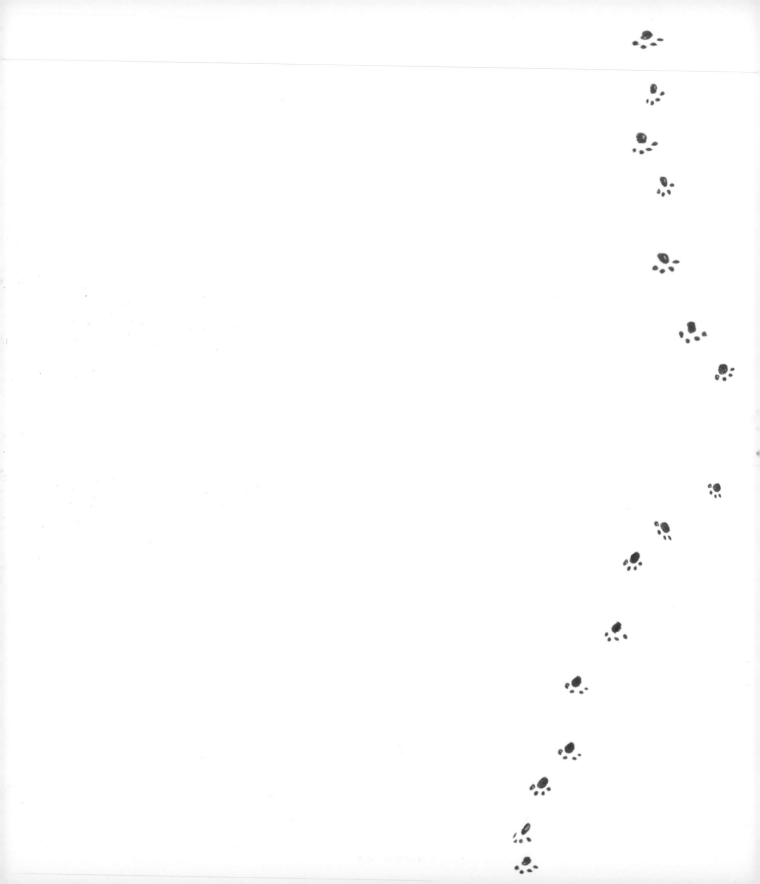

The Good Dog

and the Bad Cat

written by Todd Kessler   illustrated by Jennifer Gray Olson

Coralstone Press

Published by Coralstone Press, Inc.
New York, NY
www.coralstonepress.com

For ordering information or special discounts for bulk purchases, please contact Coralstone Press, Inc., 235 Park Avenue South, New York, NY 10003, or info@coralstonepress.com.

Illustrations by Jennifer Gray Olson
Layout by Joanne Bolton

The good dog and the bad cat: Vol. 2 of The good dog series

Library of Congress Control Number: 2015920389

Kessler, Todd, author.
The good dog / written by Todd Kessler ; illustrated by Jennifer Gray Olson. -- First edition.

pages : color illustrations ; cm

Summary: When a mysterious thief is hiding in the Lee household and store, little puppy Tako is assigned the task of uncovering the mystery. Although Tako succeeds in exposing a thieving cat that has been hiding in the house, when she gets thrown out Tako begins to have second thoughts about the consequences of his actions. Is Allie the cat truly "bad," or are there more layers of complexity to her story? Little Tako may be the only one who can uncover the real truth, but to do so he'll have to fight the vicious river rats and risk his own safety.
Interest age level: 005-010.

Issued also as an ebook.
ISBN: 978-0-9898085-1-4

1. Dogs--Behavior--Juvenile fiction. 2. Bakeries--Juvenile fiction. 3. Dogs--Habits and behavior--Fiction. 4. Bakers and bakeries--Fiction. I. Olson, Jennifer Gray, illustrator. II. Title.
[Fic] 2015920389

Printed and bound in China through Bolton Associates, Inc., San Rafael, CA 94901
10 9 8 7 6 5 4 3 2 1

For Fenn

The Happy Family Bakery was a busy place.

Tako was a good dog,
so he helped whenever he could.

He picked up things
that were dropped.

He was very quiet when
the twins took their nap.

He helped Ricky
with his homework—

and cleaned up all the crumbs ...

... especially the crumbs left for him on purpose.

Because Tako was such a good dog,
he was allowed to go on adventures
with Ricky and his friends.

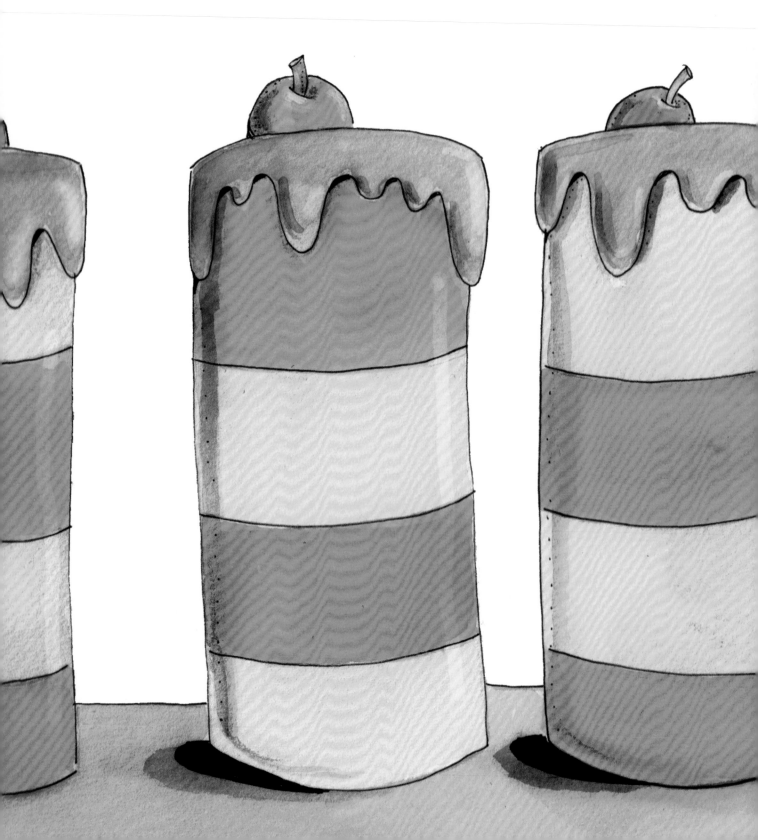

Everything was perfect.
Except for one thing.

There was a thief.

The thief stole a butterscotch bean bob—

A cherry chewbilee—

and Lia's drawing
of a blue dog.

Every day something else was missing.

"The problem here," said Papi Lee,
"is that everyone is too busy to catch the thief."

"Except Tako," Grandpa Lee added.

Tako felt bad.

He really wanted to catch the thief and protect his family.

But he wasn't sure that he could.

Every day Tako told himself,
"Today is the day I will
catch the thief."

But whenever he guarded one thing ...

... something else
would disappear!

One day Tako found a clue.

He followed the little footprints,

but they just ...

... ended.

Tako lay awake that night.

He wondered who
made those prints.
Where were they hiding?
Why were they stealing
from the Lee family?
Why were they so bad?

He heard strange
pitter-patter sounds
that frightened him.

Next morning Tako decided he wasn't going
to be afraid anymore.

He would set a trap to catch the thief.

So Tako gathered some things he knew the
thief liked to steal ...

... and he hid.

Then he heard something ...

Tako leapt out and barked.

The thief was a cat!

A very bad cat.

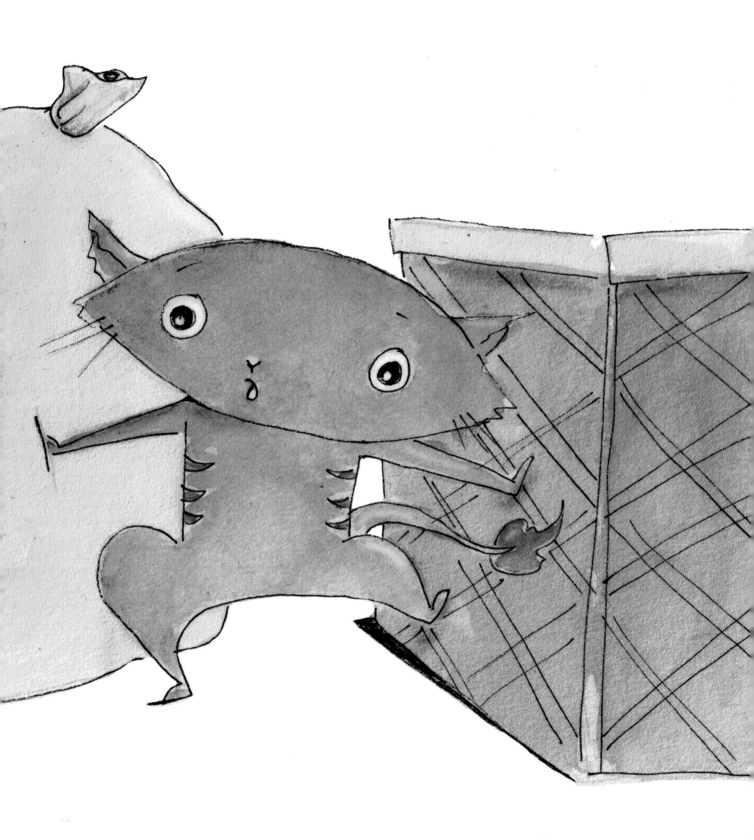

"Tako has caught the thief! Yay!"
Ricky shouted.

"This bad cat has been stealing lots of things from us,"
said Mimi Lee.

"Baddy kitty katty!" said Mia and Lia.

"Now you go away,
bad cat, and don't ever
come back here!"
Grandpa Lee shouted.

As a reward for being
such a good dog,
Papi Lee gave Tako
a whole, warm,
smushberry muffin.

That night Tako slept soundly.
The thief was gone.

The world was a good place again.

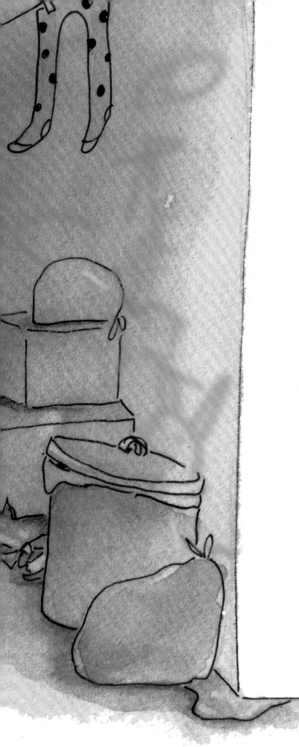

Next day Ricky and Tako walked by Lulu's market.

"That bad cat used to hide in my alley, and she stole things from my store," Lulu said.

"Don't worry," said Ricky. "Tako will protect our neighborhood from that bad alley cat."

The alley was just the kind of dirty, messy place where a bad cat would hide, Tako thought.

But she wasn't there, and Tako was glad.

On the way to play soccer
Tako saw something moving.

He growled.

"Look, it's that bad cat!" Ricky said.

"I'm going to call you Allie because
you lived in an alley!" Ricky told her.

Tako barked.

"Forget about her, Tako!" Ricky said. "She's not stealing
things from our house anymore. Let's go play soccer!"

Tako tried very hard,
but he couldn't forget
about Allie the bad cat.

He wanted her to go away ...

... far away.

Then the ball got kicked off the field, and Tako forgot about Allie.
Chasing the ball was Tako's favorite part of the game.

There was Allie, looking as if she didn't care about anybody.

It made Tako so mad!

He barked and charged at Allie.

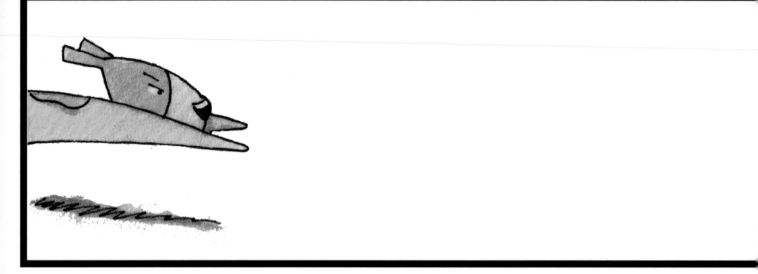

But Tako was going so fast he couldn't stop!

Allie didn't seem afraid.

She hopped to the side.

When everyone saw Tako they started laughing.
"Look at Tako!" they said. "He fell into a hole!"

As Ricky lifted up Tako, he saw Allie.
She seemed to be laughing too.
It was all her fault!

Tako was mad.

Next day when Ricky was playing soccer, Tako went exploring
... well, he wasn't really exploring. He was looking for that bad cat.

And then he saw Allie, just lying in the sun ...
as if she didn't care what a bad cat she was.

Tako would show her!

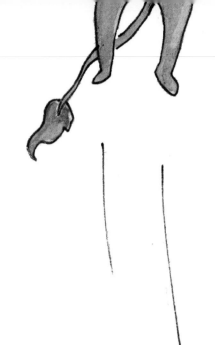

Tako jumped.

Allie was very mad—

but to Tako she looked very funny!

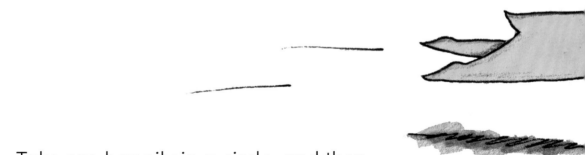

Tako ran happily in a circle, and then
dashed back to the soccer game.

Next day Papi Lee made cherry chewbilees
for Ricky and his friends to eat after the game.

Tako was being a very good dog. He wasn't nibbling on the chewbilees, even though they looked delicious, and he was guarding them from that bad cat.

What was that sound?

Tako barked and chased Allie
all the way down to the waterfront.

Tako was going to get those cherry chewbilees back and let that bad cat know she could never steal from anybody again.

Suddenly Allie stopped.

Then Tako saw why Allie had stopped ...
she was surrounded by river rats!

They were the meanest, scariest animals
Tako had ever seen. Allie dropped the
chewbilees and growled at the rats.

Allie jumped over the water to another rock
and ran away.

Then the rats saw Tako.
Tako ran as fast as he could.

He wished he could jump high like Allie.

For the rest
of the day
Tako stayed
very close
to Ricky.

He was
worried
that the
river rats
were
following
him.

That night Tako couldn't sleep.
He was thinking about Allie.
Where did Allie sleep now?
She would have to be somewhere high,
so the river rats couldn't get her.

Then Tako started to wonder
where Alllie had slept when she was
hiding in the Lee home.

Maybe she slept somewhere high
here too, in a place where her enemies
couldn't get her.

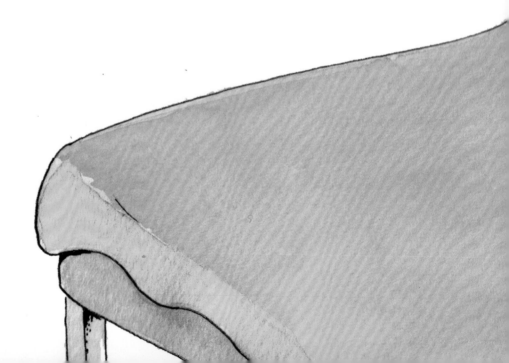

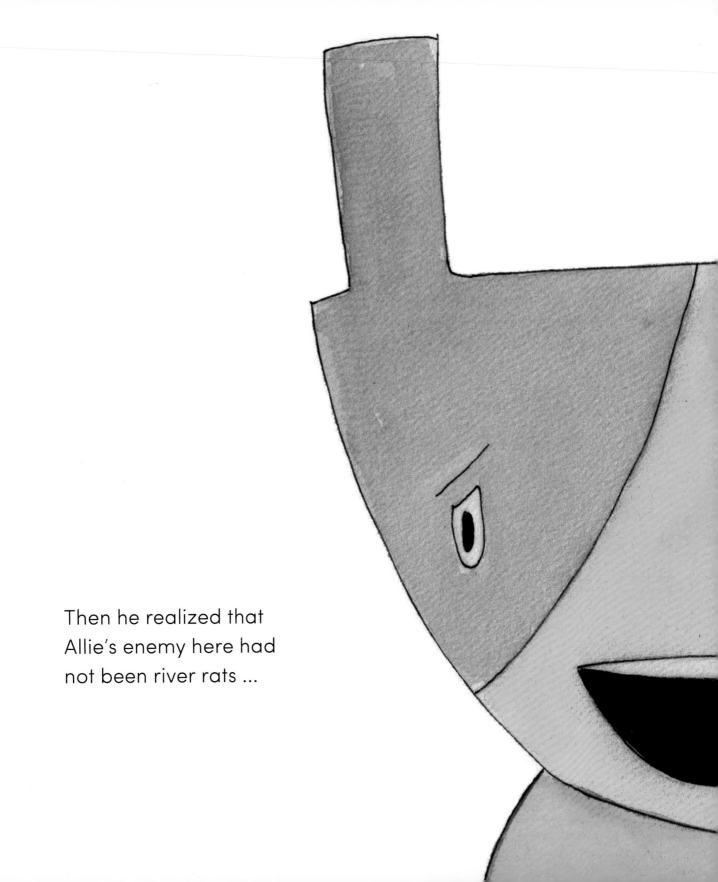

Then he realized that
Allie's enemy here had
not been river rats ...

... her enemy had been Tako.

Tako looked for Allie's old hiding place.

Then he saw a hole in the top of the closet.
It looked like the kind of place where a bad cat
would like to hide.

Tako was curious.

He wanted to see that bad cat's
dark, messy hiding place.

But what Tako found was
not what he expected.

It wasn't a dark, messy place at all.
It was a little home.

Tako remembered when he was little
and lived alone in a box before Ricky found him.
More than anything Tako had wanted a real home.

Maybe Allie had just wanted a real home too.

Tako stayed awake all night worrying about Allie. He hoped the river rats wouldn't get her.

Next morning Tako wasn't hungry.
He didn't eat any of his breakfast.

Mimi Lee thought he might be sick.

"Maybe Tako shouldn't play soccer today,"
said Papi Lee.

Tako jumped up, barked, and wagged his tail eagerly. Everyone laughed.

"Tako wouldn't miss a soccer game for anything!" said Ricky.

While everyone played soccer,
Tako wandered along the waterfront looking for Allie.
But she wasn't there.

Then he saw Allie's tail!

Allie was growling and swiping at the river rats with her claws.
But this time there was nowhere to jump.

Tako ran up and barked at the rats
to scare them away.

But the rats weren't scared of Tako.

Allie jumped away,
and she fell into the water.

But Allie couldn't swim!

Tako jumped into the water
and swam quickly towards Allie.

Tako wanted to help Allie.
But Allie thought he was chasing her,
so she tried to get away.

Allie splashed with her paws.

The more she splashed, the more she sank.
Finally Allie disappeared under the water ...

... and she was gone!

Then suddenly Tako felt something on his back—

little wet paws!

Tako swam back to shore as fast as he could.
The rats came charging towards them.

Tako and Allie barked and growled.

Ricky and his friends heard the noise and came running.

"Look!" they shouted. "Tako and that cat are fighting the rats!"

Tako, Ricky and Allie worked together
to chase away the rats.

"You're right," said Ricky, "Allie is hurt.
We have to help her."

Ricky told the story of how Tako and Allie
fought off the rats.

Mimi Lee cleaned Allie's leg,
and Papi Lee wrapped it with a bandage.

"Can Allie stay with us now?" asked Ricky.

"Allie was a bad cat and a thief," Grandpa Lee said.
"I don't think it's a good idea if she stays here."

Tako barked at Grandpa Lee.

Grandpa Lee was surprised.

Everyone clapped.

"Tako is a good protector dog!"
Papi Lee exclaimed.

Mimi Lee said, "If Allie can be a good cat now,
we might let her stay."

Ricky sat next to Tako and Allie. "Tako is a good dog, so he will help Allie be a good cat," he said.

And Allie wanted to be a good cat too,
so she helped whenever she could.

She picked up things
that were dropped.

She was very quiet
when the twins took
their nap.

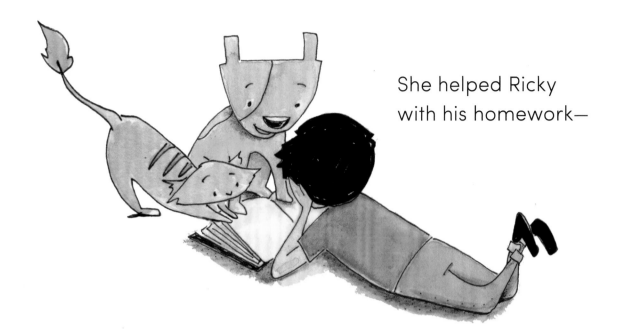

She helped Ricky
with his homework—

and she cleaned up all the crumbs ...

... especially the crumbs left for her on purpose.

Tako knew he would help Allie
be a good cat, so she could have
a warm home too—

and they could be friends forever.

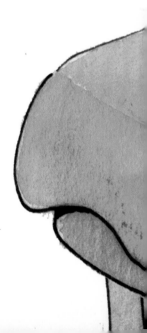

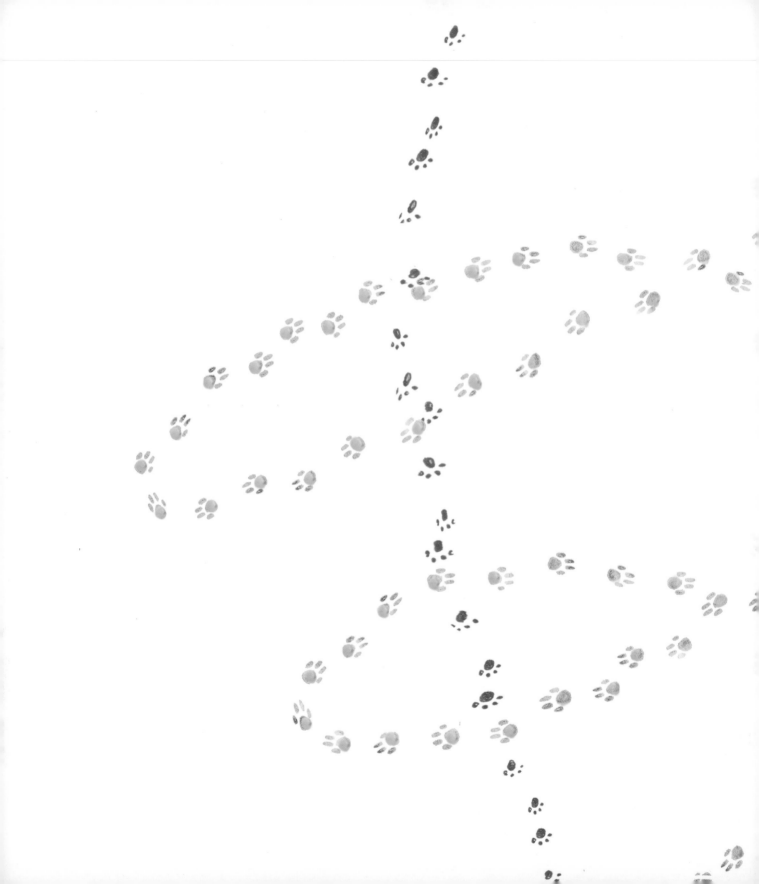

THE END

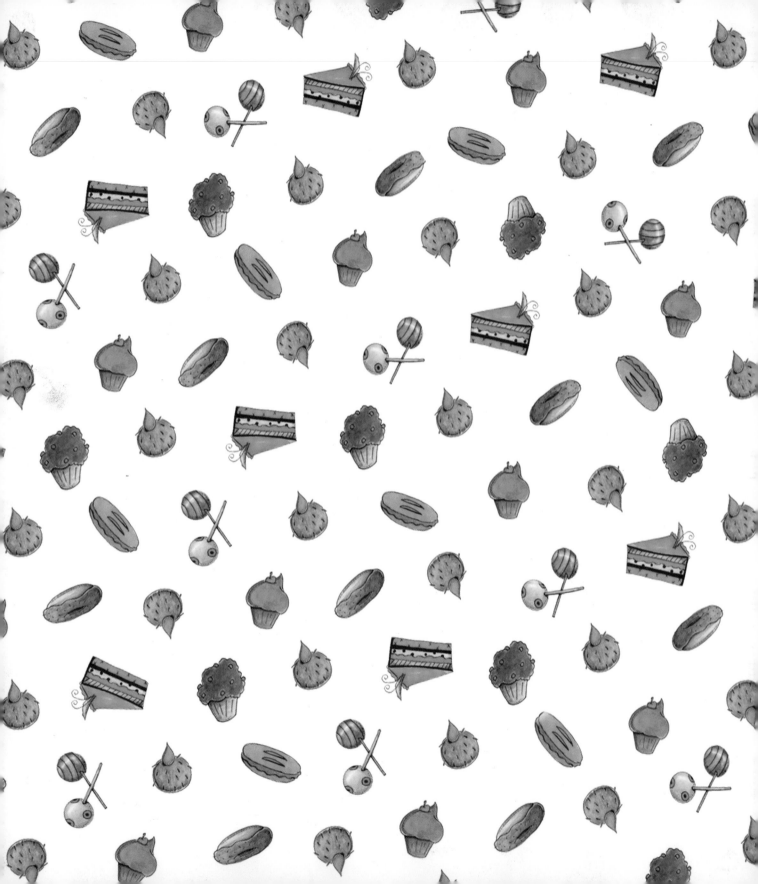